I am dedicating this book to my parents because of their unconditional love. My mother was a lead educator in her career and community, and I always admired her will. She will always be my guiding light in education leadership, and without her tenacity, I do not know where I would be today. My father was a lawyer, a non-fictional published writer, and a great public speaker. My father used to read stories to us and specifically chose books that related to us. My father will always be my role model in guiding others towards the best forms of themselves through logic and reason.

I would like to dedicate this book to my colleagues and professors because of their persistence in implementing inclusive curriculums in their safe-space classrooms. My professors educated me to promote anti-bias education and a culturally relevant curriculum to strengthen learning processes. Thank you to Dr. M. Murray, Dr. H. Reynolds, Dr. G. Navarro-Cruz, Professor M. Andrade, and Dr. E. Haywood-Bird.

Both of my children were born and raised in the USA, and it was my mission to find books that supported their personal experiences as first-generation American Pakistani Muslims. Unfortunately, I could not find enough books while I was raising my children. Since then, I voraciously set my path to write children's books to promote diversity, equity, and inclusion. A huge thanks to my son, Temoor, who has been my strength since he was born. He inspires everyone with his integrity, caring nature, and calm personality. This graduate brilliant young man is succeeding in the technology field. A very special thank you to my daughter, Natasha, for her support and guidance in this process. Natasha pushed her educational trajectory from a small-town elementary school to graduating from Yale University as a first-generation American Muslim. Her passion and determination supported her goals, and she always made room to support her classmates, local community, and friends. Thank you Temoor, and Natasha, for paving the way for future children to reach their dreams.

Published by TNWINC.

Library of Congress Control Number 2021905408

Natasha Prepares for Ramadan

By

Tasneem Sana Khan

Today is a special day! The first day of Ramadan is tomorrow, and Natasha is preparing with her family. Ramadan is the ninth month in the Muslim lunar calendar. During this time, Muslims fast worldwide, and they do not eat or drink from sunrise to sunset. The moon helps Muslims predict when the month of Ramadan begins and when it ends.

With Ramadan around the corner, there is so much to do! Six-year-old Natasha heads downstairs. She runs to the family room, and sees her Mom decorating the house with "Ramadan Mubarak" on sparkling banners with moons and stars. Natasha loves to help her family, especially during the month of Ramadan.

After helping her Mom put up decorations, Natasha runs to her Dad's coffee corner. Natasha's Mom and Dad typically make coffee for themselves at the start of the fast, also known as Suhoor.

Suhoor is when Natasha's family wakes up before sunrise to eat healthy and energy-packed meals to start their fast. Iftar is at Sunset when they break their fasts with dates and other delicious foods.

Dates are chewy brown dried fruits that taste almost like candy! Dates have an essential role during Ramadan, and Natasha's parents say that they provide vitamins for our bodies.

Natasha and her older brother Temoor are excited to fix the Ramadan calendar. It has thirty surprise tasks, and each day they will do a good deed such as watering the plants, feeding their dogs Buddy and Charlie, and more! The calendar also includes a Prayer Chart with the five daily prayer timings all Muslims must complete.

Natasha's Mom shows her a to-do list, and Natasha begins to dance because the first thing on the list is to create her favorite food-Samosas! Every Ramadan, her family sits around the table and makes hundreds and hundreds of mini Samosas. A Samosa is a triangle-shaped pastry that can be baked or fried and filled with yummy meats and potatoes. Natasha and her family head to the grocery store to pick up all the ingredients to make Samosas and other yummy foods!

Natasha and her family drive to their favorite market. Natasha stays with her Mom, and they head to the fruit and vegetable aisle, while Natasha's Dad and Brother head to the meat section. After they pick up their groceries, Natasha and her brother pick out their favorite ice cream.

Natasha's parents like to cook a variety of healthy meals during Ramadan. One of Natasha's favorite drinks is Rooh Afza; a rosewater syrup served with water or milk. Natasha and her brother help put away the groceries and prepare the Samosa station.

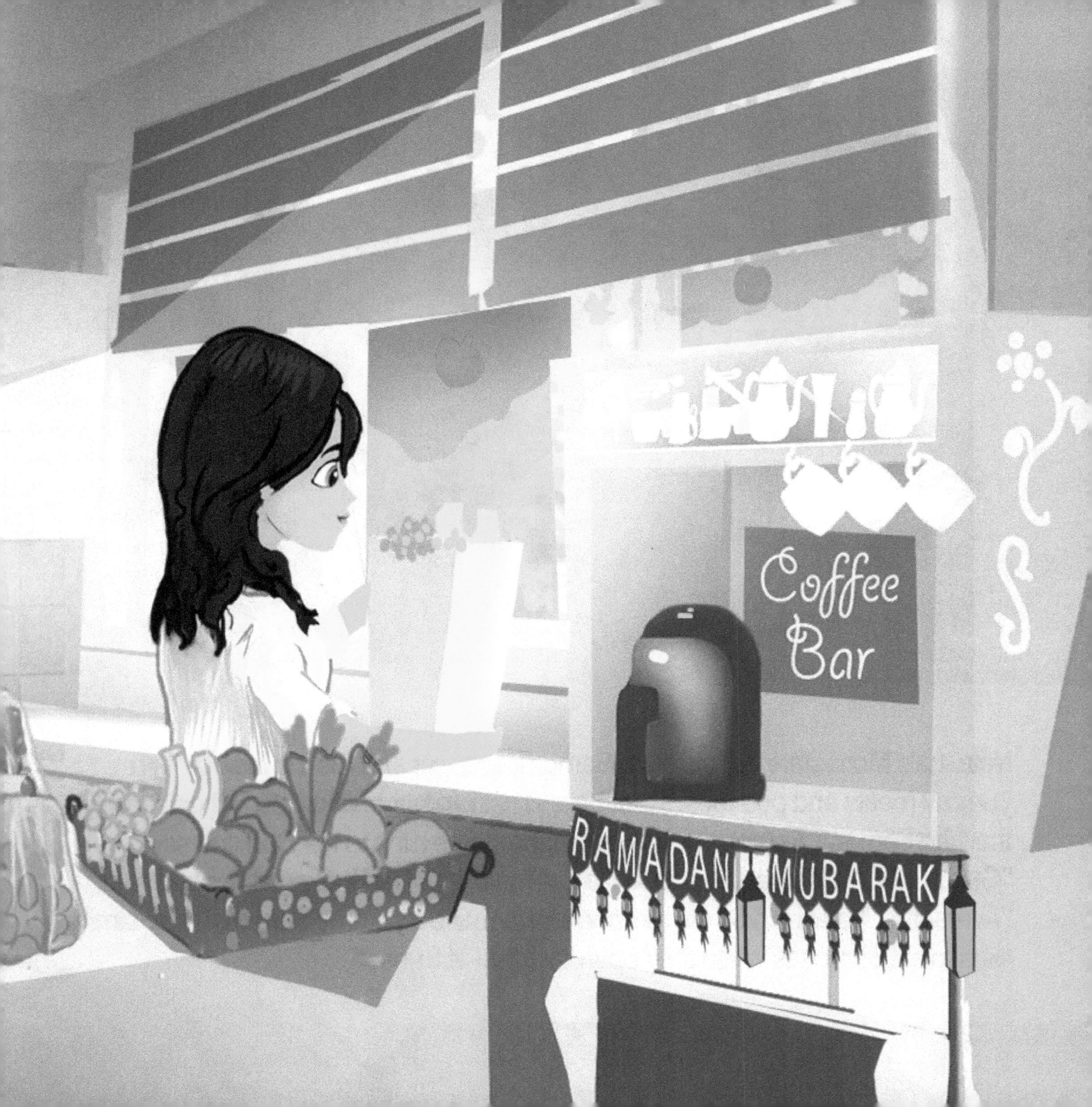
Coffee Bar
RAMADAN MUBARAK

Natasha's Mom starts to fold each Samosa wrapper and fills the insides with yummy meats and potatoes. Natasha and her brother quickly follow her lead. By the 10th Samosa, Natasha became an expert! She runs to her Dad and says, "Guess what? I learned how to fold a Samosa." Her Dad looked at her and said, "Awesome, Natasha, you sure know how to make a yummy Samosa!" Her family likes to eat Samosas when they open their fast at Sunset!

As Natasha and Temoor finish wrapping Samosas Natasha's Mom is scurrying around the kitchen. Natasha's Mom finishes cutting fruit, vegetables, and baking her famous Tandoori Chicken. "We are almost ready!" says Natasha's Mom. Ramadan is a huge part of religion, and the foods we eat are a big part of the culture!

After they finish decorating their home and preparing food for Ramadan, Natasha and her brother run to their backyard to pick apples. Each year, Natasha's Family creates Ramadan Celebration Baskets for their neighbors including fresh fruit from their backyard.

Natasha and her brother begin to fill the baskets with a box of moon-shaped cookies, mint tea bags, apples and a jar of dates. Natasha's Dad always says that sharing food is a generous gesture that they should do year-round, especially during Ramadan. As they wrapped up the gifts, Natasha's Dad leaves to drop them off at each home. When he returns, they head to the Mosque to listen to the Quran and pray a special prayer called Taraweeh.

In Ramadan, there is a special prayer called Taraweeh. During Taraweeh, Muslims listen to the Quran. The Quran is a holy book written in Arabic and divided into thirty parts. When they arrive at the Mosque, Natasha follows her Mom to the prayer room. An hour passes, and they complete their prayers for the night. Natasha looks at her Mom, and her Mom says, "Let's go home. We have great plans for tomorrow." Natasha couldn't help but smile because tomorrow is the first day of Ramadan.

AUTHOR'S NOTE

As an educator, my student's observations have been my favorite assessment tool. I use their input for my curriculum development to create a vibrant and dynamic classroom. I decided that it was my journey to create representation in the children's book community. Our classrooms depict human diversity. Our students come from different ethnicities, nationalities, religions, and more. It is the educator's job to celebrate this diversified society. Our responsibilities as teachers are to strengthen children and serve as a liaison to the real world.

ABOUT THE AUTHOR

Tasneem Sana Khan is an educator, and California Polytechnic
University, Pomona Alumni. She is on the path to earn her Ph.D.
program in Education Curriculum and Instructions. She is also
a published author and columnist. Her first book "Asslamalekum
America," published in 2006 and received recognition internationally.
She currently lives in California with her husband, two children, two
dogs, Charlie and Buddy. Her hobbies are traveling, volunteering with
environmental organizations, painting, and cooking different types of
cuisines.

CPSIA information can be obtained
at www.ICGtesting.com
Printed in the USA
BVHW061258270621
610448BV00009BA/2185